A WEEKEND WITH WENDELL

BY KEVIN HENKES

SCHOLASTIC INC.

New York Toronto London Auckland Sydney
Mexico City New Delhi Hong Kong Buenos Aires

For Nancy and Iggie

ISBN 0-439-68620-2

12 11 10 9 8 7 6 5 4   5 6 7 8 9/0

Printed in the U.S.A.   40

First Scholastic printing, September 2004

The art was prepared as full-color watercolor
paintings combined with black pen-and-ink line.
The typeface is Baskerville.

On Friday afternoon Wendell's parents dropped him
off at Sophie's house.
"Wendell's going to spend the weekend with us," said
  Sophie's mother, "while his parents visit relatives out of town."
"Oh boy!" said Wendell.
  Sophie didn't say anything.

After a snack, Sophie helped Wendell carry his sleeping bag and suitcase upstairs.

"Well, what are we going to do now?" asked Wendell. "Do you have any toys?"

Sophie pointed to her toy chest.

"Is that all you've got?" said Wendell. "I've got a million times more than that. What else is there to do around here?"

"We could play house?" said Sophie.

"Only if I can make the rules," said Wendell.

So they played house and Wendell made the rules.
He was the father, the mother, and the five children.
Sophie was the dog.

Then they played hospital.

Wendell was the doctor, the nurse, and the patient.

Sophie was the desk clerk.

When they pretended they worked in a bakery,
Wendell was the baker and Sophie was a sweet roll.
"Isn't this fun?" said Wendell.
Sophie didn't say anything.

At dinner Wendell said that he was allergic to anything green—so he didn't have to eat his vegetables.
And then, when Sophie wasn't looking, he scooped the whipped cream off her dessert.

"When is Wendell leaving?" whispered Sophie.

"Soon," said her mother.

"Soon," said her father.

After Sophie's parents tucked Sophie in her bed, zipped
Wendell in his sleeping bag, kissed them both, and
turned off the light, Wendell grabbed his flashlight and
shone it right in Sophie's eyes.
"SEE YOU TOMORROW!" he said smiling.

Sophie shut her eyes. "I can't wait for Wendell to go home," she said to herself.

On Saturday morning, when Sophie woke up, there was
a lumpy blue monster jumping up and down on her
bed. It was Wendell.

She felt something pinch her leg at breakfast.
It was Wendell.

She heard scary noises coming from the broom closet.
It was Wendell.

Wendell used Sophie's crayons and left them on the
porch so they melted.

At lunch Wendell finger-painted with his
peanut butter and jelly.
"Isn't this fun?" said Wendell.
Sophie didn't say anything.

"When is Wendell leaving?" whispered Sophie.

"Soon," said her mother.

"Soon," said her father.

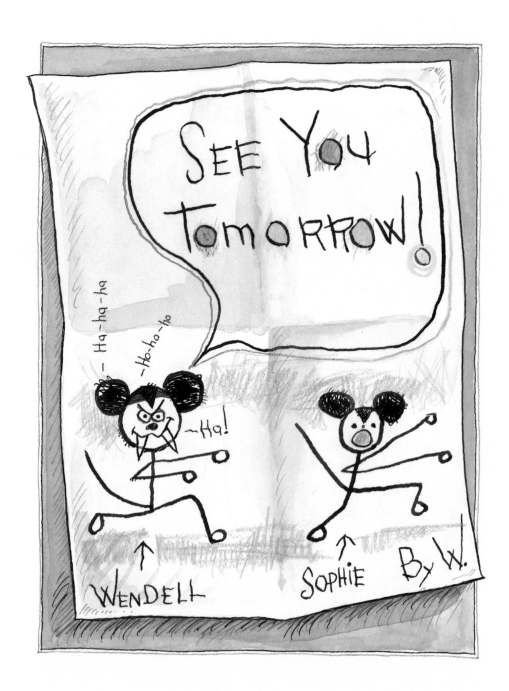

At bedtime, when Sophie put her head on her pillow, she heard something crunch. It was a note from Wendell. It said, "SEE YOU TOMORROW!" Sophie shut her eyes. "I can't wait for Wendell to go home," she said to herself.

Before Wendell's parents picked him up on Sunday morning, he tried to make a long-distance call,

he wrote his name on the bathroom mirror
with toothpaste,

and he gave Sophie a new hairdo with shaving cream.

"Want to go outside to help me wash this off?" asked
Sophie. "We could play fire fighter."
"Oh boy!" said Wendell.

So they played fire fighter—and *Sophie* made the rules.
She was the fire chief. Wendell was the burning building.
"Isn't this fun?" said Sophie.
Wendell didn't say anything.

"Do I get to be the fire chief?" asked Wendell.

"Maybe," said Sophie.

Soon Wendell and Sophie didn't care who was
the fire chief or who was the burning building.

"Time to go!" said Sophie's mother.

"Time to go!" said Sophie's father.

"Already?" said Wendell.

"Already?" said Sophie.

"When is Wendell coming back?" asked Sophie.

"Never!" said her mother.

"Never!" said her father.

That afternoon, when Wendell unpacked his suitcase, he heard something crunch. It was a note from Sophie. It said, "I HOPE I SEE YOU SOON!"